Boone

April Renner Curtsinger

ISBN 978-1-64416-210-1 (paperback)
ISBN 978-1-64416-212-5 (hardcover)
ISBN 978-1-64416-211-8 (digital)

Christian Faith Publishing, Inc.
832 Park Avenue
Meadville, PA 16335
www.christianfaithpublishing.com

Printed in the United States of America

To God who made it possible for me to do far more than I could have ever imagined. To him be the glory in this endeavor.

To my mom and first editor who will forever be my biggest cheerleader. Thank you for always believing in me and supporting whatever I do.

Hi, my name is Boone. This is the story of how I found my fur-ever home—before I even became "Boone." I was just a puppy and didn't know life could be so much better until I found my new home.

It was almost Christmas when my owners took me for a ride in their car. Christmas was all the kids had talked about because they were excited about getting new toys. Suddenly, as we rode along, the car stopped on a hill full of houses and somebody opened the car door. I thought I was just being let out to go potty. I jumped out, did my business, and spun around, hoping to get a pat on the head for being a good boy. That's when I saw the car driving away! I was so confused—and kind of scared. I sat down and waited a long time for them to come back. Finally, it started to get dark and cold. Then it started to rain. I decided I should go find a dry place.

As I walked, I started thinking, *Maybe my owners don't want me anymore. Maybe they aren't coming back.* I know I'm smelly and itchy. My hair grows a lot and gets matted. My ears hurt, and I know it costs money to take me to the vet to get medicine. I had heard my family saying all those things. But I have so much love to give! I can be their best friend if they'll just give me a chance. And let's face it… I'm a blast and extremely adorable!

I had walked and walked, and my legs were getting tired. My tummy hurt from hunger. I went to nearly every house on the hill, hoping someone would let me into their home to warm up and give me something to eat. But no one was outside in this weather, and no one came to the door. I didn't know what to do. I was all alone.

Suddenly I remembered—God could help! I looked up into the night sky and prayed, "Hey, Big Guy, I could really use your help. Can you help me find someone who wants me? I'd sure like a nice home for Christmas."

Suddenly, a white curly dog with wings and a halo appeared in the night sky above me, the area around him glowing. I rubbed my eyes, not believing what I was seeing. I said, "Who are you? Are you God? I knew it! God is a dog too! Of course, he is!"

The dog replied, "No, I'm an angel. God sent me. You asked for help, didn't you? He always hears our prayers. My name is Scooter."

"Well, nice to meet ya, Scooter. Do you know where I can find a warm, dry place for the night? And maybe a big juicy cheeseburger?" I asked.

Scooter laughed. "Well, I don't know about a cheeseburger, but I have something even better for you."

"Better than a cheeseburger?" I was confused! What's better than a cheeseburger?

Pointing over the hill, Scooter replied, "Just over that hill there's a yellow house with the back porch light on. They'll help you for tonight. They have a daughter who used to be my person. Her name is April. She rescued me from a shelter. Being hers was the best time of my life. We did everything together. We took long walks, snuggled on the couch, took car rides. She even took me to the pet store and bought me toys and treats. About a month ago, it was my time to go to heaven and I had to leave her. Her heart is still broken, and she just prayed this very night for a new dog that needs her love. She said it was all she wanted for Christmas and that she knew God would send her a dog that needed her when the time was right. Well, my friend, the time is right! It's your lucky day!"

"Really?" I said. "That sounds kind of…perfect! Can I go to her NOW?"

Scooter explained, "Well, she lives in another town, but go to the house, and she'll come see you tomorrow."

I said, "Thank you very much, Mr. Angel, I mean, Mr. Scooter, I mean…"

"My pleasure." Scooter smiled. "Give her a little lick on the cheek for me, would ya? And be a good boy."

I waved good-bye to Scooter, the angel dog, and trotted off over the hill toward the yellow house. I saw the back porch light on and walked up to the back door, peeking inside the window. I whimpered when I saw the warm light of the fireplace and the soft cozy rug.

A man came to the door. "Well, look what we have here," he said as he opened the door. "Hi, little fella! I guess you're cold. Let's get you in out of the rain. Nana, look here. Here's a little dog for April."

Nana came into the room, surprised to see me. "Well, hi there!" she said. "Papaw, let's get him dried off and get him something to eat. I'd better check with the neighbors and make sure he's not lost. If no one claims him, I'll call April and see if she wants to come down and see him tomorrow."

Well, I must be in the right place, I thought. *Little white curly dude said April would love me. Now where's that cheeseburger?*

I tried to hop up on the couch when Nana said, "Not so fast, little guy! You are too wet and muddy for the couch. I'll make you a bed in the garage."

Nana and Papaw took me to the garage and made me a nice, soft bed with blankets. Then Papaw set a bowl down in front of me and said, "Here's some ham, Pudgie. Sorry we don't have any dog food."

My eyes lit up, and my mouth watered. It smelled so good! "No problem, sir! Ham is ju-u-u-st fine! This looks delicious!" I told him by happily wagging my tail.

After eating all the ham I wanted, I curled up on the warm bed and thanked God for leading me here. Then I closed my eyes and slept…and slept…and slept.

Later I learned that Nana had texted a picture of me to April after I'd gone to bed, saying, "Look who just showed up at my house. No one is claiming him. I think he's a stray. Do you still want a dog?"

April exclaimed, "I just prayed for this tonight! I'll be there first thing in the morning!"

Then, as the story goes, April told her son, Luke, that a little stray dog showed up at Nana's and that she was going to go get me the next morning. She told him she thought God had sent them a little blessing just in time for Christmas. She asked Luke what they should call me, and he said they should look up names that mean "blessing." Apparently, the name "Boone" means blessing. Imagine that. Just a few hours ago I was dropped off on the side of the road, feeling like no one wanted me. Now someone not only wants me, but considers me a blessing from God. It's a miracle!

The next morning I woke up with sunlight coming through the window and feeling refreshed. About that time the door opened, and there she was. I knew as soon as I saw her that this was the one. This was April. My new person.

"Oh my goodness! You are so-o-o cute!" April exclaimed. "Can we call you Boone? Because you're our little blessing! I'm going to take such good care of you!"

I wagged my tail and batted my eyes as if to say, "Sweetheart, you can call me whatever you like. Just keep scratching my head like that."

"Shew!" she held her nose. "The first thing we're going to do is get YOU in the bathtub!"

After the disgraceful bath, we took a long ride to April's house and she let me sit in her lap all the way home. It was late when we got to my new home, but I got to meet my new "brother," Luke. He was fun. I had to sleep on blankets in the bathroom that first night. Something about me being stinky, and I might have fleas? Hmmph!

The next day we had to go to the vet. I'd never been to the vet. April said the vet would make me feel better. I'd been so happy to get warm and get my tummy full that I hadn't even thought about my ears hurting or my skin itching.

We walked into the vet's office, and the man in the white coat said, "Hi there, Boone. Nice to meet you. Let's get a look at you."

He shined a little light in my ears, eyes, and mouth, then looked at April and said, "Well, he's still a pup. Maybe not even a year old. He's not been treated very nice, I'm afraid. He's too skinny, has a bad infection in both ears, needs dewormed, and has a skin condition making him itch. It should get better with nutritious food and special shampoo that can heal his dry skin. Just wash him once or twice a week in this shampoo, give him this worm medicine, and put these drops in his ears. I'll go get the shots ready for his vaccines."

I cowered down behind April, and she said, "It's okay, Boone. It'll be over really quick, and you're going to feel so much better."

The vet walked in with a needle, and I backed away, saying, "Now wait a minute, I think there's been a *big* misunderstanding here. I feel F-I-N-E, fine! Really. I've never felt better."

Riding in the car afterward, I guess I looked defeated. April giggled and patted me on the head. "I think I know what will cheer you up, Boonie Boone."

We pulled into a pet store. April put me in a shopping cart.

"Let's get you a few things…let's see…we need some healthy yummy dog food, treats, a couple of squeaky toys, a collar and leash, and a dog bed," she said as she put each thing in the cart beside me.

"I don't really need the dog bed. I can just sleep in that big cozy bed with you." I batted my eyes as sweetly as I could.

At the cash register, April got me a special Christmas cookie shaped like a candy cane.

We went home and snuggled on the couch together. The next day was going to be Christmas Day. When it was time for bed, April laid my new dog bed on the floor beside her bed and sat me on it.

"It's time for bed. This is where you sleep, Boone." She patted the bed.

I looked at it with my saddest puppy dog eyes, trying to convince her I should just sleep with her.

"You'll be fine. I'm right here." She laughed.

We said our prayers, both bowing our heads. Then I peeked up at her over the edge of the bed.

April smiled and said, "Oh, all right. Get up here. I guess it *is* Christmas Eve after all."

I snuggled in beside her, smiling contently. We woke up on Christmas morning, and they opened presents with pretty paper. I got to tear up the paper, and I even had a few presents of my own! Afterward, we had to get ready and take that long drive again to Nana and Papaw's house for dinner. I hoped Papaw had more of that yummy ham he gave me last time. There were lots of other people there this time, and everyone played with me and snuck me ham and turkey under the table. I curled up under the beautiful lights of the Christmas tree, my belly and heart full. I felt so very loved and thankful for my new family. I might have been their blessing, but they are mine too.

About the Author

April Renner Curtsinger grew up in Mt. Vernon, Kentucky, a small rural town where people wave when they pass you on the street and everyone knows your name. She attended Eastern Kentucky University and received a degree in child development. She has a love for children's books and animals, mainly the ones with fur. She combined the two, with their simple, light-hearted innocence, in her first attempt at writing. April now lives in Elizabethtown, Kentucky, where she enjoys spending time with both her human family and the furry ones alike.